ISBN 0 00 171216 0
Copyright © 1973 by Dr. Seuss and A. S. Geisel
A Bright and Early Book for Beginning Beginners
Published by arrangement with Random House, Inc., New York, New York
First published in Great Britain 1974
Printed in Great Britain
Collins Clear-Type Press: London and Glasgow

The SHAPE of ME and OTHER STUFF

By Dr. Seuss

A Beginning Beginner Book

COLLINS AND HARVILL

You know . . .

It makes a fellow think.

The shape of you

the
shape
of
me

the shape
of everything I see . . .

a bug…

a balloon

a bed

a bike.

No shapes are ever quite alike.

Just think about
the shape of beans

and flowers

and mice

and big machines!

Just think about
the shape of strings

and elephants.....................

..................and other things.

The shape of lips.

The shape of ships.

The shape
of water
when
it
drips.

Peanuts

and

pineapples

noses

and

grapes.

Everything
comes
in different shapes.

Why, George!
You're RIGHT!

And...
think about
the shape of GUM!

The MANY shapes
of chewing gum!

And the shape
of smoke
and
marshmallows
and
fires.

And mountains

and

roosters

and

horses

and

tires!

And the shape of camels..........

.....................the shape of bees

and the wonderful
shapes of back door keys!

And the shapes
of spider webs

and clothes!

And,

speaking of shapes,

now just suppose...!

Suppose
YOU
were shaped
like these...

...or those!

...or shaped
like a BLOGG!

Or a garden hose!

Of all
the shapes
we MIGHT have been...

I say, "HOORAY
for the shapes we're in!"